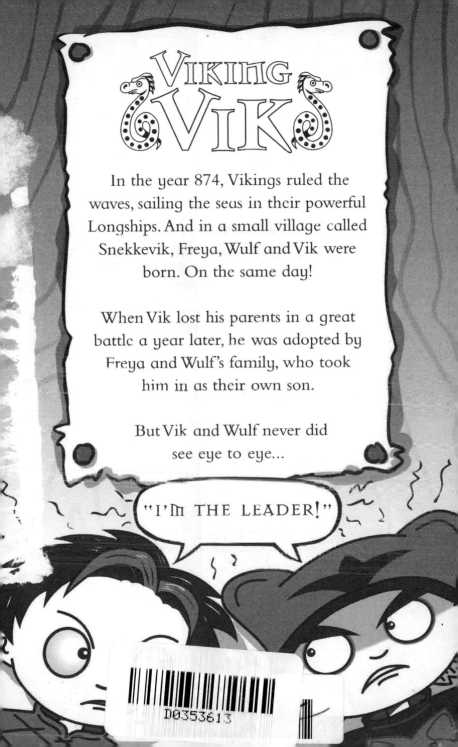

# VIKING VIK

In the year 874, Vikings ruled the waves, sailing the seas in their powerful Longships. And in a small village called Snekkevik, Freya, Wulf and Vik were born. On the same day!

When Vik lost his parents in a great battle a year later, he was adopted by Freya and Wulf's family, who took him in as their own son.

But Vik and Wulf never did see eye to eye...

"I'M THE LEADER!"

FOR EVA

First published in 2008 by Orchard Books
First paperback publication in 2009

ORCHARD BOOKS
338 Euston Road, London NW1 3BH
*Orchard Books Australia*
Level 17/207 Kent St, Sydney, NSW 2000

ISBN 978 1 84616 721 8 (hardback)
ISBN 978 1 84616 729 4 (paperback)

Text and illustrations © Shoo Rayner 2008

The right of Shoo Rayner to be identified as the author and
illustrator of this work has been asserted by him in accordance with the
Copyright, Designs and Patents Act, 1988.

A CIP catalogue record for this book is available from the British Library.

1 3 5 7 9 10 8 6 4 2 (hardback)
1 3 5 7 9 10 8 6 4 2 (paperback)

Printed in Great Britain

Orchard Books is a division of Hachette Children's Books,
an Hachette Livre UK company.

www.hachettelivre.co.uk

# VIKING VIK

## AND THE SECRET SHIELD

## SHOO RAYNER

ORCHARD BOOKS

"I hate beans!" Vik sighed, as he popped open another pod and emptied it into the bowl.

"Never mind," said Gran.
"When you've finished this lot,
you can go out and play."

"Can you tell us a story, Gran?" Freya asked. "Shelling beans is so boring. Tell us a story about when you were little."

"Yeah!" Vik perked up. "Tell us one about my mum and dad."

"Your dad!" said Gran, with a little laugh. "He was a one. Sometimes I think he was too brave for his own good."

Vik couldn't remember his real mum or dad. He only had stories to remind him of them. However much Wulf and Freya's mum and dad treated him as their own son, he still felt different.

"I remember the time your father escaped from the Dwarves," Gran said. "He must have been the same age as you are now."

Vik's eyes grew wide with interest. "Oh yeah?" he urged. "Tell us that one!"

"It was the day he and Jarl Magnusson climbed up to the Mountain Gate," Gran began. "You know – that cave which is supposed to lead into the Mountain Kingdom.

"That's where the Dwarves live and have their forges, where they make swords and armour and jewellery."

Gran told them how Vik's dad, Harald, was the only one brave enough to go into the darkest part of the cave.

"Something happened in there."
Gran's voice dropped to a hushed
whisper. "There was a howling and
a wailing and a clashing of wood and
steel, then Harald ran out of the cave,
yelling that the Dwarves were after him.

"He and Jarl were so terrified, they ran like the wind, all the way home. That's when Harald lost his shield. He always had his shield with him in those days."

"What happened?" Vik asked breathlessly.

"Harald said the Dwarves caught him but he managed to fight his way free. They never dared go up to the Mountain Gate again." Gran shelled the last bean pod. "OK, you can go and play now!"

"Anyone coming with me?" asked Vik.

# VIKING FOOD

Viking food has to last on long sea voyages and through long dark winters. To preserve it, the food is either pickled, salted, bottled or rotten!

**Pickled Gherkins**

**Salty Cod**

**Bottled Beans**

**Rotten Reindeer Meat**

"Where?" Wulf asked, tossing stones in the dust. He sounded bored.

"Up to the Mountain Gate, of course!" said Vik.

"It sounds a bit dangerous," Freya said, nervously. "We can take a lantern with us," Vik suggested.

"OK, then. If we must," said Wulf, who was now sounding bored to hide his fear of being captured by the Dwarves.

Vik found a lantern and lit a new candle inside it. They would have to be careful not to let it go out as they climbed up the mountain.

Vik called to his dog.
"Come on, Flek. Let's go!"

"Do we have to go in there?" Freya eyed the cave mouth anxiously.

"You'll be all right," Wulf said, cheerfully. "We'll protect you, won't we, Vik?"

Vik and Flek were busy examining the Mountain Gate. The mouth of the cave was triangular and about ten feet high.

Vik had the feeling that someone, or
something, had been there quite recently!
Could it really be the Dwarves?

Was this really the
doorway to the
Mountain Kingdom?

"OK, stick together," Vik ordered. Although Wulf was bigger than him, Vik felt that this was his expedition – he was in charge.

# DWARVES

*Dvergar*, or Dwarves, live underground in the Mountain Kingdom.

They are very clever and are famous for their skills in metalworking and jewellery-making. They can also cast powerful magic spells.

*Dvergar* are fierce fighters, so don't make one angry!

Inside, the cave opened up into a large chamber. The first thing they noticed was the runes scratched onto the rocky walls.

Vik's fingers traced the spiky shapes. "*Dvergar,*" he whispered. "It means Dwarves! This is the right place."

"Oooh!" Freya whimpered. "I'm scared!"

"Phwoar! What a stink!"
Wulf complained.

There was a scuttling noise above
their heads. Freya gripped Vik's arm.
"What's that?"

Vik held the lantern up high.
Hundreds of tiny eyes watched
them from the ceiling. "It's only
bats," Vik said calmly.

"I hate bats!" Wulf grumbled.

27

Vik put his foot in something soft and squelchy. He lowered the lantern. "Urgh!" The ground was covered in bat poo. The stinking piles were alive with small creatures that scrambled over the surface.

"Waagh! Spiders!" Wulf's
cry alarmed the bats.
Suddenly the cave filled
with tiny flapping,
squeaking creatures.

Flek barked and snapped as
they swooped past his head.

"I'm not staying here!" Wulf cried, running towards the bright light of the cave entrance.

"Neither am I!" screamed Freya, as she ran after Wulf and joined him in the sunshine outside.

"Looks like it's just you and me, Flek." Vik patted his faithful pet. The bats settled down and Flek stopped growling.

Vik wasn't frightened by some little creepy crawlies. Something was giving him extra courage. Something was calling him, drawing him deeper into the mountain…

# VIKING NAMES

Vikings name their children after famous people or dead ancestors.

Viking surnames come from the father's first name.

Vik's dad was called Harald, so Vik's surname is Haraldson, which means son of Harald.

Freya's dad is called Jarl, so her surname is Jarlsdóttir, which means Jarl's daughter.

The cave became narrower at the back. The runes scratched on the walls told him someone had been there before.

With Flek close at his heels, Vik edged his way forwards into the darkness. His lantern flickered in the draught.

He was deep inside the cave
when the light reflected off
some shiny metal.

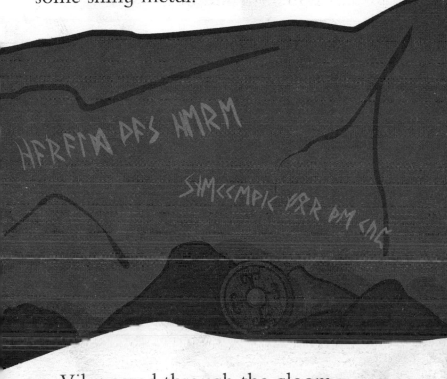

Vik peered through the gloom.
A round object leant against the
wall – maybe it was something
the Dwarves had left behind! Vik
bent and picked it up.

It was a shield! Vik brought
the lantern closer. Flek nosed
up for a sniff. It wasn't very
big, almost a toy – Dwarf-size!
Runes were carved on the
back. Vik spelt them out:
HARALD!

It was the shield his father had lost. That's what had drawn him to this dangerous place!

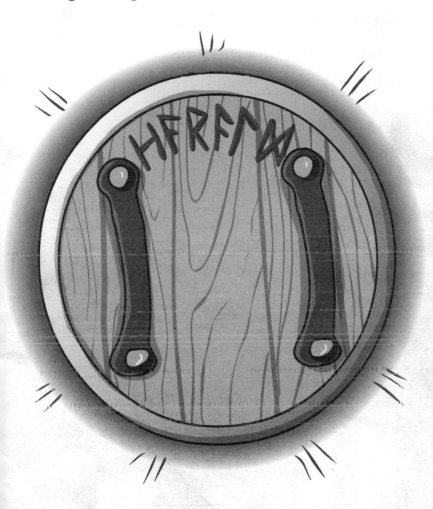

At that moment a hideous sound boomed from deep down at the back of the cave – a bellowing, groaning roar that seemed to come from the heart of the Mountain Kingdom itself.

BLEA-A-A-

Vik froze. The lantern fell to the floor. The light guttered and sputtered out. Clattering footsteps came closer.

Vik sniffed the air. "Goats!" he said aloud. "I'd know that smell anywhere!" The footsteps stopped. Flek growled. He could smell a goat in the dark, too.

A-A-ARGH!

"Ba-a-a-a-a-ah!" Vik
yelled into the darkness.
"Yap! Yap!"
Flek barked.

The goats panicked and ran back
to the dark part of the cave where
they had been lurking.

"Goats!" Vik laughed. "I bet there never were any Dwarves. I bet the Mountain Kingdom is just an old story. But no one needs to know that, do they – eh, Flek?"

Vik edged his way through the darkness until he came to the mouth of the cave. He could see Wulf and Freya waiting outside.

Somehow, he knew for certain that his father had played a trick all those years ago. Now it was his turn.

Vik ran from the cave holding up his father's shield and yelling at the top of his voice. Flek followed, barking wildly.

Wulf and Freya looked terrified.

# RUNES

**Runes are the Viking alphabet.**

| | | | |
|---|---|---|---|
| ᚠ | ᚢ | ᚦ | ᚨ |
| f | u | th | a |
| ᚱ | ᚲ | ᚷ | ᚹ |
| r | k | g | w |
| ᚺ | ᚾ | ᛁ | ᛃ |
| h | n | i | j / y |
| ᛇ | ᛈ | ᛉ | ᛊ |
| e | p | z | s |
| ᛏ | ᛒ | ᛖ | ᛗ |
| t | b | e | m |
| ᛚ | ᛜ | ᛟ | ᛞ |
| l | ng | o | d |

"Look!" Vik shouted.
"I got my father's shield
back from the Dwarves,
but they're coming
after me — run for
your lives!"

"That's definitely your father's
shield," Gran said, as she watched Vik
carve his own name next to his
father's. "I remember him carving
those runes just like you're doing now."

Vik strapped the shield to his arm, raised his wooden sword and waved it above his head.

"Nothing frightens Vik Haraldson!" he roared defiantly.

Gran watched Vik with a gentle fondness in her eyes. "You really are just like your father," she said quietly. "Yes, just like him, and just as brave – but not too brave for your own good, I hope!"

### SHOO
### RAYNER

### All priced at £3.99

The Viking Vik stories are available from all good bookshops,
or can be ordered direct from the publisher:
Orchard Books, PO BOX 29, Douglas IM99 1BQ
Credit card orders please telephone 01624 836000
or fax 01624 837033 or visit our internet site: www.orchardbooks.co.uk
or e-mail: bookshop@enterprise.net for details.

To order please quote title, author and ISBN
and your full name and address.
Cheques and postal orders should be made payable to 'Bookpost plc.'
Postage and packing is FREE within the UK
(overseas customers should add £2.00 per book).

Prices and availability are subject to change.